Once upon a time, seven kingdoms ruled the world. Each one controlled an element: fire, light, ice, water, earth, wind, or shadow. These may not be the elements you know, but our world is very different today. To maintain the cosmic balance, each of the ruling kingdoms was granted only a piece of a powerful relic called the Elemental Pendant. Over time, people forgot why the fragments were kept separate and guarded jealously by the royal houses.

They knew only that uniting the relic could destroy the world.

To the kingdom of Calabast went the right half of the Soulstone, a fiery red ruby of unparalleled beauty.

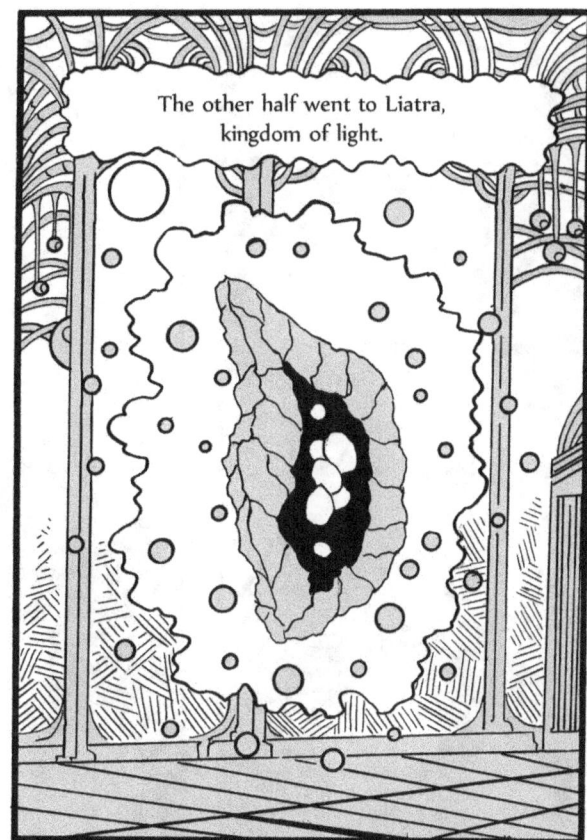

The other half went to Liatra, kingdom of light.

The right and left halves of the lovely sapphire, Lifestone, went respectively to the ice kingdom of Istra...

...and the water kingdom of Rileth.

Heartstone, a piece of jasper, went to the earth kingdom of Tarnul.

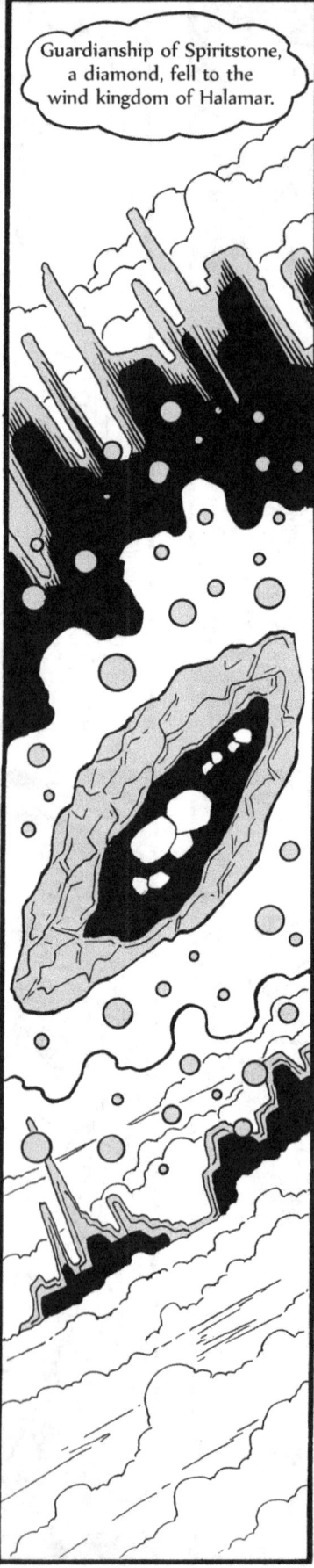

Guardianship of Spiritstone, a diamond, fell to the wind kingdom of Halamar.

Shadestone, of course, went to Quintessa, kingdom of shadow. The history books are divided on the subject of Shadestone. Some depict the fragment as an emerald while others speak of a chunk of onyx.

For a thousand years, relative peace existed. There were minor skirmishes to be sure. Calabast would turn their trebuchets against the ice walls separating it from Istra, rewriting their borders for a time.

Liatra or Quintessa would invade Rileth for water supplies.

Halamar would turn loose the wild winds on the simple earth folk of Tarnul. But by and large, none of the kingdoms had a reason to fight each other, so they each prospered.

Do not become weary with the names of so many kingdoms. That is less important than the events set in motion by an ambitious sorcerer named Draygor. After mastering his craft and excelling seemingly everywhere, he set out to unite the seven kingdoms under a single banner, his own.

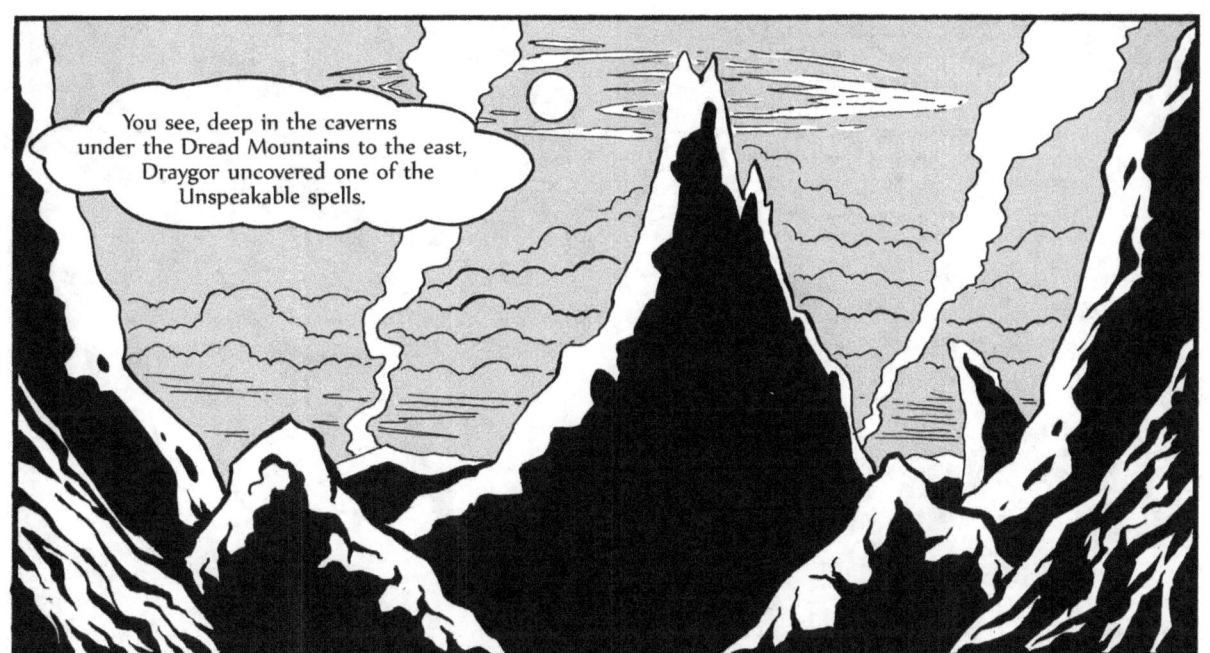

You see, deep in the caverns under the Dread Mountains to the east, Draygor uncovered one of the Unspeakable spells.

This gave him the power to control the dragons.

In essence, he became king of the dragons

It's quite an impressive title and a very important job, but Draygor quickly tired of ruling the scaly beasts. They were not his people, so they could not truly appreciate the power he held over them.

At first, he tried war, but he had no head for the nuances of strategy required to win. Instead, his dragons attacked unsuspecting villages, burning and destroying at random.

This, of course, provoked the kingdoms to raise up armies to fight the dragons.

The Great Dragon War, as it is called today, lasted three years before Draygor abandoned it.

But he did not surrender his desire to rule the hearts of men.

Instead, he turned to trickery and the Wildwood Witch, the only being whose power he sort of respected.

Using the last wealth of his fading kingdom, Draygor hired assassins to kill the heirs to the seven kingdoms...

...and placed a curse upon the royal families. This curse prevented all royal couples from bearing children. But he didn't stop there.

Draygor traded the Wildwood Witch control over dragons for control over the minds of men. One may wonder why she agreed to such a poor deal, and the answer is simple: she too wanted a child. The continuous use of magic over the years had rendered it impossible for the Witch to gain a child through normal means. Draygor uttered many sweet promises, but he had no intention of giving his rival a human child who might one day grow up to become a threat to him. When the time came for Draygor to pay the Witch, he gave her a single scroll that contained a dragon's soul. Then, he enslaved her mind and forced her to participate in his wicked scheme.

When the kingdoms exhausted other means, Draygor let it be known that the Wildwood Witch might have the answer to their prayers.

No kingdom would admit anything was amiss, but one by one and quite in secret, the queens of each kingdom traveled to the Wildwood Forest and sought out the Witch.

Under duress, the Witch granted each queen a potent potion that would give them one child and restore their ability to bear other children.

Instead of fashioning a child for herself, the Witch wove the dragon soul into her current work.

The price for such power was steep indeed.
The queens surrendered the Words of Power protecting their piece
of the Elemental Pendant.

They comforted themselves with the knowledge
that nothing could be done unless the seven random phrases could be said at once in the right order.
Thus, each queen became pregnant within days of each other, and in the due course of time,
seven princesses were born.

Why princesses?
Draygor's stint as king of the dragons gave him ample time to study and read. The stories that mattered to him focused on the idea of sacrificing innocent princesses along the path to power. Every world-conquering manuscript he could obtain also reinforced this idea.
The plan he came up with required much patience.

Not big on this virtue, Draygor created a potion that would allow him to sleep for seven years. When that wore off, he whipped up a new batch and slept for another seven years. Although tempted to do so again upon his second awakening, Draygor refrained.
The princesses had just passed their fourteenth birthdays. It was time to start collecting them.

He wasn't certain he needed all seven but having spares couldn't hurt. Once the relic was restored to its full glory anyone could wield its power, but according to Draygor's research, only members of the royal houses could safely touch the fragments of the Elemental Pendant while they remained pieces. The ancient prophecies and texts glossed over important details like whether or not the royals of one house could handle the fragments entrusted to another kingdom. Sloppy work to be sure, but none of the scribes were alive enough to bother punishing.

At least the scribes agreed that the royal being touching the enchanted precious stones must be sixteen. That gave Draygor two years to plot and plan. He needed every moment to bolster his supply of control spells...

...for he found that the power he'd stolen from the Witch had some severe limitations and loopholes. He couldn't control every situation, but he wanted to be as prepared as possible.

Finally, the princesses celebrated their sixteenth birthdays. The major kingdoms rejoiced and sent invitations to the lesser kingdoms. Princes flocked to each party, hoping to win over a fairheart—and the kingdom said fair heart would one day inherit.

Draygor let them bask in the triumph of successfully raising a princess to the age of majority before striking. By exerting his mind control over the Wildwood Witch again, Draygor regained some influence over the dragons. It paled against the power he once wielded, but he managed to coordinate several strike teams.

Using more deliberate strokes this time and having learned much from his past mistakes, Draygor systematically went to war one kingdom at a time.

He also made one significant alteration to his strategy. Instead of seeking to beat the kingdoms into complete submission, Draygor quickly struck deals with each of the royal houses. He demanded only their firstborn child, the princess granted life by the Wildwood Witch's potion.

Though saddened by the prospect of losing their Crown Princess, each tiny kingdom, except the shadow kingdom of Quintessa, comforted itself by knowing that they had several other heirs on whom to place their hopes and dreams.

Calabast surrendered first, followed quickly by Liatra, Istra, Rileth, Tarnul, and Halamar. Within two months, only Quintessa's princess, Melia, remained free

It surprised no one when Draygor's dragon army and conscripts drawn from the other six kingdoms arrived at Quintessa's southern border. They met no resistance and simply marched into the heart of the kingdom.

When they came within sight of the royal castle, every soldier braced for a bloody conflict. Draygor's forces had found Quintessa's army. Every inch of the walls and fortifications brimmed with soldiers waiting to defend their small royal family to the last man, for unlike the other kingdoms, Quintessa had no spare heirs yet. One was in the works, but he wouldn't show up for at least another seven months.

Deep within the castle, down in the dungeons, Princess Melia conducted her own negotiations with the stable boy, who unknowingly held the world's fate in his profusely sweating palms.

Denny, you know this isn't right.

Tis fer yer own safety, milady,

The king will hand yer decoy over and the dragon king will go on his merry way. I'm not to let ya out until late tomorrow evening.

. . .

Who is it?

. . .

Niala or Aisha might pass for her in looks, but they didn't have the protection of royal blood.

If Draygor followed the same pattern as he had in the six fallen kingdoms, he would make the "princess" retrieve the enchanted stone from the hidden room of the royal vaults. Without royal blood, Melia's decoy would surely perish.

Tugging against the shackles with all her might only left her sore in addition to being stuck. As she leaned against the wall, a new restlessness settled upon Melia, making her skin itch. The distant sound of drums beat softly in her ears.

Duum Thump Duum Duum Thump

Do you hear that, Denny?

Hear what, milady?

Twisting her hands around so she could grip the chains, Melia gently pulled on the bonds in time to the slow, steady cadence of each drumbeat still marching through her head.

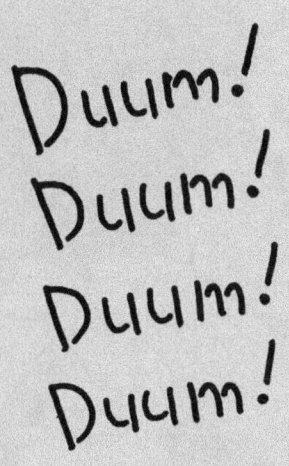

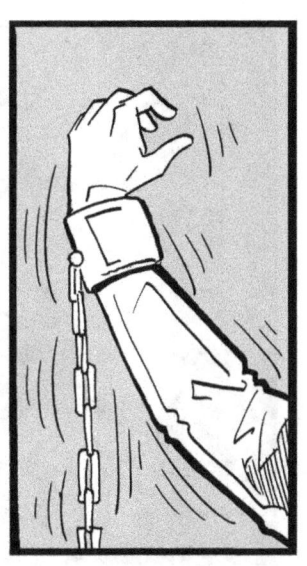

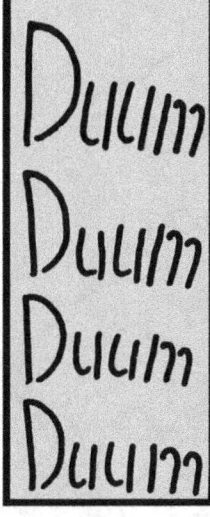

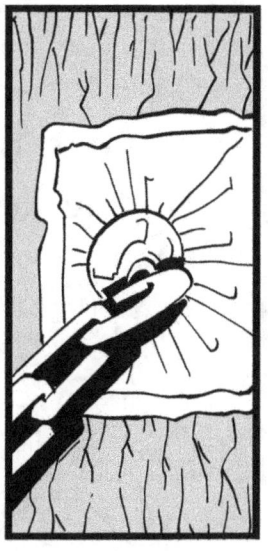

She had to get upstairs to the throne room quickly or lose one of her very few friends. The path to the throne room from the dungeon wasn't familiar to her, but Melia had the advantage of Denny's echoing cries to follow. Once she made it to the main floor, the path grew more familiar.

Instinctively, she drew up the cowl on the dark robes she wore. She had meant to go meet the invaders at the city gates and stop this madness before it began, but her parents —and eight royal guards—had intervened, throwing her into the dungeons "for her safety."

I am who you seek.

Convincing Draygor of her identity proved much harder than the young princess anticipated. Both the king and the queen babbled nothing but denials...

...until Draygor ordered them to stop speaking and had the command backed up with physical gags.

Niala played the part of princess very well, from gorgeous emerald dress right down to an air of aloofness that takes years of practice.

Why would this ragged child claim to be the princess if she is not?

Many offered answers, but they blended into one incoherent stream of noise.

. . .

Because she wants you to go away.

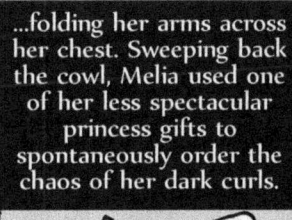

...folding her arms across her chest. Sweeping back the cowl, Melia used one of her less spectacular princess gifts to spontaneously order the chaos of her dark curls.

Any sorceress could do that...

I am the princess! Send this imposter away!

I need Quintessa's real princess to do me a favor, and I do not have much time to waste on trivialities like imposters. I need the princess alive, but she does not need all her limbs. Tell me quickly which is which or they both lose a hand.

That one is the princess.

You will complete the task I've set before you or become orphans in the next hour.

I suggest you work quickly.

Three quarters of an hour passed while the seven princesses tried different combinations. Laying out the pieces of their fragments was not the issue. The problem came when speaking the seven sets of Words of Power in the correct order.

They tried every combination possible, and still failed.

Every time they failed, the pieces would fly back into their hands, forcing them to start over.

How is that possible!

YOU...

...fetch the Wildwood Witch!

!?!

Why did they fail?

Unbind me and you shall have your answer.

What is it?

I believe it is glitter, my sister.

It is the Glitter Shroud.

It will send these Daughters of Fate into the Shadowlands where the Elemental Pendant may safely be forged.

. . .

!!!

What just happened? Where did she go?

The Glitter Shroud is gaining strength, my lord. Have patience and you will have your answers.

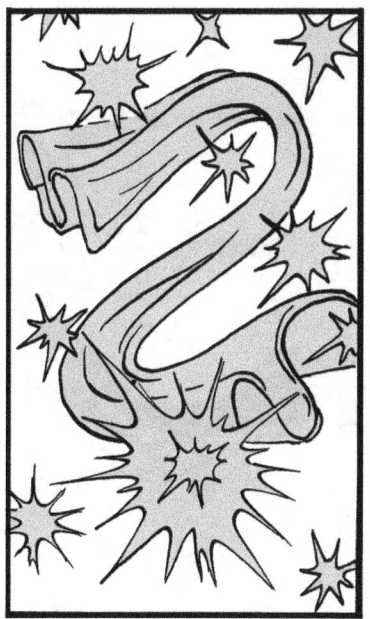

And what did the
Shroud gain
this time?

The Glitter Shroud
received resilience,
milady.

And what will it
gain from me?

From you it will
receive wisdom.

Do it...

...

How come she gets to keep her body?

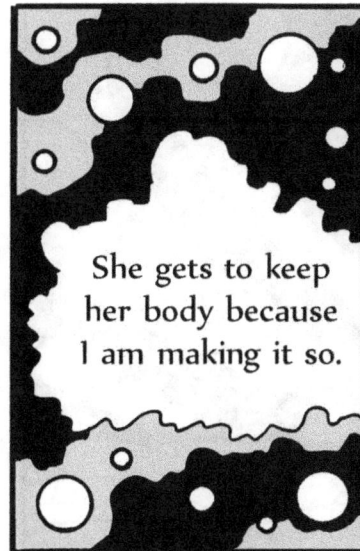

She gets to keep her body because I am making it so.

Peace, Shadow Princess.

It's the White Witch.

Come again?

Listen closely, Daughters of Fate. Time is short and much is at stake.

If we wish to right wrongs done, all must leave self behind and become one. You have the pieces. You have the words. You have the will, and I have the way. What do you say?

Speak plainly please ...

Stand there and wait for the spirit orbs to join ya, sweetheart.

. . .

They looked more like blobs to Melia, but she shrugged.

Only by your combined powers and blah blah blah do we get out of this joint and save the world, so work with me here.

Oh, this is stupid.

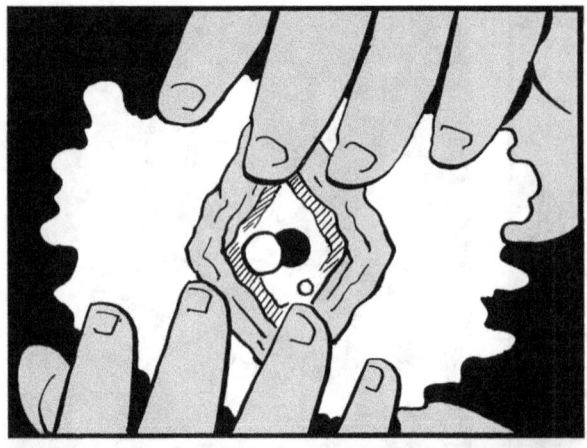

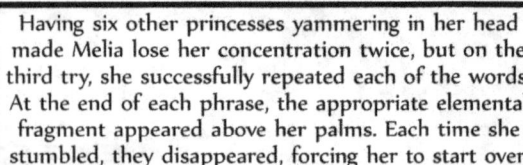
Having six other princesses yammering in her head made Melia lose her concentration twice, but on the third try, she successfully repeated each of the words. At the end of each phrase, the appropriate elemental fragment appeared above her palms. Each time she stumbled, they disappeared, forcing her to start over.

In order, the phrases unlocked the pieces for water, earth, fire, light, shadow, wind, and finally ice. "Now bring the fractured pieces together," instructed the White Witch, once certain the fragments would stick around.

Melia almost asked how, but she felt the others working through her. Letting most of the pieces continue to float, she gripped both bright red halves of the Soulstone. The sensation that flooded Melia was akin to Rhonda and Sia solemnly clasping hands. The ruby halves united in a quick, dazzling display of fire and light.

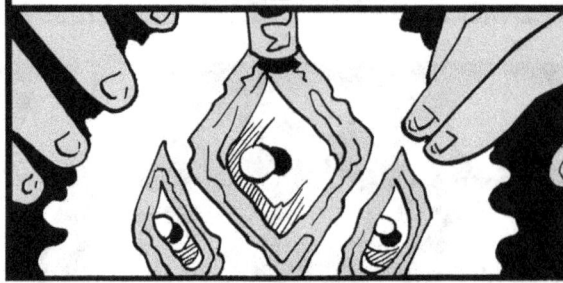

A similar union happened for the sapphire, Lifestone. Heartstone and Spiritstone continued to slowly circle above Melia's hands. When she was ready for them, they nestled onto the thin onyx backing of Melia's Shadestone. After every fragment fit like a puzzle, Melia brought the emerald green section of Shadestone down upon it.

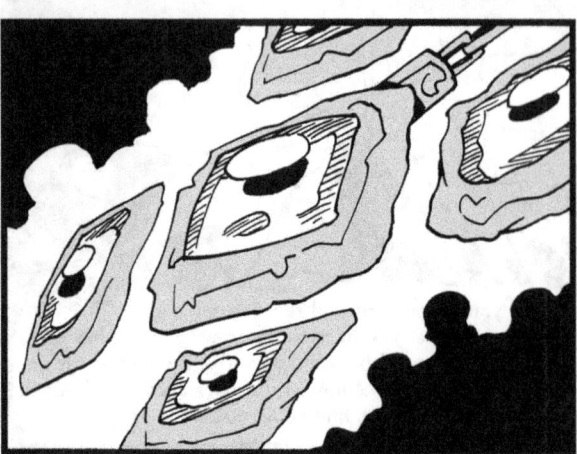

No sooner had the Elemental Pendant formed in full, Melia found herself back in the mortal world, but not in her usual body.

As a child, Princess Melia used to have very vivid dreams of flying, but nothing compared to the actual sensation of hovering above an enthralled—and terrified—crowd in her parents' throne room. Worse, even as a baby dragon, she nearly filled the space by the ceiling.

Bonk!

...

The princess spirits, still trapped inside Melia, offered conflicting advice of varying levels of usefulness. Talia screamed. Kenja expressed concern for the effects of falling debris on the crowd below. Anne cried. Sia said to fly high enough to break free and Rhonda demanded she land before something got permanently damaged.

The resulting internal turmoil made Princess Melia want to hurl ...

... but she refrained because it would not be ladylike in such a public forum.

Of the masses below, Draygor recovered first. Stretching forth his hands and concentrating very hard, he attempted to exert mind control over Melia, but with the Witch still unconscious, his powers had faded.

Melia felt Draygor's efforts like a gnat repeatedly flying into her face.

She tried to protest, but instead blasted a stream of fire that scorched the ceiling.

Dismayed that his first attempt failed, Draygor retrieved the scrolls of his most precious spells from an inner pocket of his dark robes. With trembling hands and voice, he read the words of Dominate Dragons ...

... a spell that should let him control any nearby dragons for at least half an hour. The effects were immediate. Princess Melia calmed down and hovered a safe distance from both ceiling and floor. Even as she outwardly settled, a fierce battle ignited inside her mind.

The magic behind the spell made the words extremely compelling. Melia found herself agreeing that obeying Draygor was the only sensible thing to do. Fortunately for Melia—and the world—the other princesses trapped in her head would have none of that.

Rhonda set off little fireballs to snap Melia back to reality

Talia fought Draygor's spirit form with conjured icicles. Sia changed the level of light rapidly and repeatedly to disorient their enemy.

Anne sent wind everywhere so that he had nowhere to hide within the confines of Melia's mind.

Kenja and Haya worked together to channel life-sustaining strength into Melia's spirit.

In short order, the princesses defeated and cast out Draygor's presence.

That should have been the end of it, but then, the dragons showed up, ready to fight for Draygor.

He had accidentally added the wrong amount of toad's blood and snail slime to the spell bound to his scroll. Instead of .1 mL of each, he added .01 mL, and that is a lesson on checking your numbers carefully. Significant figures matter. Thus, the duration of his dragon control spell suffered along with its potency, but the range increased exponentially. It also had the side effect of teleporting the eager dragons to the skies above Quintessa.

Realizing he had a formidable dragon army awaiting his every command, Draygor cackled in triumph.

Melia shuddered as her heightened dragon senses delivered the madman's decree. She tried to respond but couldn't figure out how to make her mouth form the words. The results were very much like a puppy trying to catch a butterfly. The sight of a baby struggling so adorably melted even the firmest of dragon hearts. They stared, transfixed for almost a full minute. Some even cooed, trying to comfort the youngling.

A chorus of mental praise and encouragement rose from the dragons.

Realizing they had an audience, Princess Anne instructed Melia on how to keep their attention.

Melia performed flips and barrel rolls, blew tiny puffs of fire, and generally showed off for a solid two minutes.

Some of the princesses protested, but not Anne. She flashed out of Melia's dragon form and swept down to inhabit her own body. The transfer process for the others occurred over the course of the next minute.

Some believe Draygor watched so closely that he forgot to kill the Queen Gwendolyn, but it's more likely the White Witch stayed his hand. When the last princess spirit had left her, Melia descended slowly and spontaneously changed back into her human form.

The shell of herself that had been left when they first entered the Shadowlands disappeared like smoke.

What are you talking about?

Can I please eat him?!

Be patient!

That is what I'm talking about. Little one, you must choose whom to serve. The humans have many a leader, but we dragons have none. Come, fill that role. Be our queen.

The deep male voice reverberated in Melia's chest. The large red dragon named Zarnoth flooded her with a brief history of the strife between the dragons and the humans. If she went with them and became their queen, she could usher in an age of peace.

"Why me?" Melia asked in wonder. Her heart trembled, for she knew not which path to pursue. Every dream of a quiet, uneventful life ruling a small and relatively insignificant kingdom shattered. "And what will happen to Quintessa? I am the only heir."

You are bearer of the Elemental Pendant and a shapeshifter beside. Both man and beast will listen to you. As to your homeland, you are the only heir for now, but that will change within the year.

Do I have to go with them?

Of course, you do. And once you get your royal cave system set up, you'll have to invite us all for tea. You can't very well expect to run a proper kingdom without having parties ...

Excuse me, but may I eat him now?

No, Tiberius. You'll have to make do with a fattened calf for now, but when we leave, we'll take him with us.

And if he so much as thinks of uttering another control spell, you may eat him.

My queen has spoken. I look forward to the day you slip up ...

... little snack.

www.ingramcontent.com/pod-product-compliance
Lightning Source LLC
Chambersburg PA
CBHW080818250626
47159CB00010B/3428